P9-BYT-422

DO YOU ENJOY BEING FRIGHTENED?

WOULD YOU RATHER HAVE NIGHTMARES INSTEAD OF SWEET DREAMS?

ARE YOU HAPPY ONLY WHEN SHAKING WITH FEAR?

CONGRATULATIONS ! ! ! !

YOU'VE MADE A WISE CHOICE.

THIS BOOK IS THE DOORWAY TO ALL THAT MAY FRIGHTEN YOU.

GET READY FOR

COLD, CLAMMY SHIVERS

RUNNING UP AND DOWN YOUR SPINE!

NOW, OPEN THE DOOR— IF YOU DARE !!!!

Shivers

A GHASTLY SHADE OF GREEN

M. D. Spenser

Plantation, Florida

ISBN 1-57657-046-0

EXCLUSIVE DISTRIBUTION BY PARADISE PRESS, INC.

Cover Design by George Paturzo
Cover Illustration by Eddie Roseboom

Printed in the U.S.A.
30572

To Adolph, who got us both out of there

Chapter One

"I have a feeling we're not in Kansas any-more," I said nervously to Mom.

She laughed.

"No, thank goodness!" she answered. "We've been driving for two days to get *away* from Kansas. Isn't it nice to be on a real family vacation again? It's been a whole year since the last one. And now it won't be long until we're finally at our home away from home."

Of course, the whole family wasn't there. My dad, who's a scientist, had gone on a business trip to Alaska to study new ways to drill for oil through the frozen tundra. He was going to be gone for six months, so we were taking our vacation without him.

Wherever the heck our vacation was going to be.

I looked out through my window with increasing concern.

The road we were on cut through the middle of tall coconut palm trees and dense palmetto bushes. Outside the car, everything was green.

Sometimes a long, tropical leaf stuck out so far that it brushed the side of our car, making a frightening racket as it scraped against the metal. This place was a jungle — wherever it was.

All Mom had told my little brother, Timmy, and me was that we were going to Florida for a one-week vacation. Right away, I got excited. I even kissed the lucky stone I keep on my dresser: *Yessss*! Orlando, here we come!

I thought about how awesome it would be to ride Space Mountain at Disney World and go to Universal Studios and do all that theme-park stuff.

But when Mom said we weren't going to Orlando, my excitement faded.

"How can we drive all the way from Kansas to Florida and not stop at Orlando?" I asked.

She just explained that we were going to some place even better than Disney World. We were going to an area very few people visited, somewhere natural and beautiful and exciting. She made it sound pretty cool.

So I decided, hey, maybe it wouldn't be so bad after all. Even if Mom wouldn't tell Timmy and me *exactly* where we were going.

"Be patient!" she kept saying. "I want it to be a surprise."

From the looks of this jungle, I knew we'd be plenty surprised. I was glad I brought my lucky stone along.

But I still couldn't understand why Mom had brought all her equipment from work with us. I thought we were going on vacation, not on some field expedition like the ones she sometimes takes for research.

My mom is a botanist, a scientist who studies plants. She works at a university in Kansas City but she's always going to strange places like the Amazon or Tahiti to study weird trees and shrubs.

She has a couple leather bags full of scientific equipment — flasks and test tubes and rubber hoses and all kinds of chemicals. She even carries a micro-

3

scope with her.

Now all this stuff was jammed into the back of our old Chevy station wagon, along with suitcases and coolers and wading boots and rubber rafts.

And, of course, Tannin. He's our beagle, a small, pretty dog with a gold and white coat.

Mom named him. I guess tannin is some yellow plant stuff that looks like our dog's hair.

Whatever. I thought it was a dumb name, but we were stuck with it now.

"Just two minutes and we'll be there!" Mom announced happily. "This is going to be so great! I just can't wait."

"Mommy, where *are* we?" Timmy asked. "I have to go potty again!"

I'd had to listen to this all the way from Kansas. My brother is just three years old and it seems like he goes to the bathroom every half-hour. Sometimes he doesn't make it in time and has an accident. It's so gross!

"Yeah, Mom — where *are* we?" I said. "Where's the beach? Where's the ocean? Where are the cute girls in bikinis? This doesn't look like any place in Florida I've ever seen on TV."

I'm twelve and a half, and I've seen lots of shows that take place in Florida. And there are *always* cute girls in bikinis. When you're a boy who's already in middle school, that's important.

I like girls a lot. So I figured maybe I'd meet some great girl and we could hang out at the beach together. Then this would be a really good vacation anyway — even if we weren't going to Orlando.

"Jason, just wait a minute and you'll see," Mom said to me. "You're going to love it! I promise you. It's like no place you've ever seen before — even on TV. It's wild and rough and full of strange plants and animals. But I'm afraid you probably won't find many cute girls in bikinis there."

Now I was getting annoyed.

"*Mooommm!*" I whined. "Where are you taking us?"

"Mommy, I have to go potty," Timmy repeated. "I have to go, Mommy!"

"OK, OK! Here we are boys," Mom said, turning the station wagon on to a narrow dirt road. It ran through a forest of vines and bushes and trees.

I couldn't even see the sky. "Our cabin is right at the end of this driveway."

"Driveway? This is a driveway?" I asked. "It looks like a hiking trail through the middle of Africa! You can't be serious! I haven't seen anything except huge green plants for an hour! Where are we?"

We pulled up in front of a dumpy wooden shack at the end of the bumpy road. Mom stopped the car.

I couldn't believe it! *This* was where Mom was taking us for vacation?

How could this be? This didn't even look like Florida!

It was just a swamp — a massive swamp that stretched in front of us as far as I could see. Behind us was nothing but a dense growth of tropical plants for miles and miles and miles.

"This is the place, guys!" Mom said cheerfully. "Isn't it just the coolest thing you've ever seen? A whole week at the edge of the Everglades!"

"The Everglades? What are *they*?" I asked.

"You haven't studied the Everglades yet in school? Tsk, tsk! What are they teaching children these days?" Mom said. "The Everglades is a fresh-water marsh that covers hundreds of square miles in southern Florida, Jason. They call it the 'river of grass.' And it's like no place else on earth. The water flows through the reeds and grasses here. And many species of birds and animals call this their home."

"Like I care?" I snapped.

"Like, you *should* care!" Mom said. "It's a unique environment, Jason. Wait until you see some of the things that live here. You're going to be amazed."

"*Mommy!* I have to go potty — *now!*" Timmy said urgently.

"OK, Timmy. Run over there to that little building behind the cottage. That's our bathroom. Hurry!" Mom said. Timmy raced from the car.

"Our bathroom's *outside?*" I complained. "Mom, can't we just get out of here and go to Disney World?"

"Give it a chance," Mom said. "There's all sorts of great stuff around here. Where else can you have a vacation around alligators?"

"*Alligators?*" I hollered. My uneasiness turned suddenly to fear. "Mom, are you crazy? They eat kids like me!"

"Don't be silly, Jason. This whole place is infested with alligators and they don't live off eating children," Mom explained. "You'll see all kinds of wildlife: alligators and buzzards and snakes."

"*Alligators and buzzards and snakes!*" I said, my fear growing more intense.

Alligators and buzzards and snakes! I thought. Oh, my!

"Where's your sense of adventure, Jason? I'm surprised at you," Mom said. "This is going to be like living in the pioneer days. It's going to be a vacation you'll remember all your life."

"Yeah, that's what I'm afraid of," I replied.

I was just sure it was going to be a terrible, terrifying vacation, something so awful I'd remember it all my life.

However long — or short — that turned out to be!

Chapter Two

I hated this place!

Talk about dull. There was *nothing* to do at the shack — uh, I mean, cabin — in the Everglades. Whenever I called it a shack, Mom got mad at me.

But it really was a dump, inside and out.

It had a rickety front porch with a door that led straight to the living room. Really, though, it was the *only* room, except for a tiny kitchen and two small bedrooms.

The living room had a small brick fireplace, and was furnished with a sagging red couch and two chairs that looked like they came from the Salvation Army's discard pile. There was one table and one kerosene lamp, just like people used for light in the 1800s.

The cabin had no electricity, no running water, no phone. Nothing.

And don't forget the outhouse around back.

We could see it from the bedroom Timmy and I shared. Our room had one small dresser, two narrow bunk beds and a table with a candle. I put my lucky stone on the dresser — and hoped it would make me lucky enough to leave this place alive.

Wow, talk about living in the Dark Ages! I felt like some kind of ancient explorer sent on a voyage to find new lands for the king.

It was really isolated around there, too. There was no one within twenty miles, at least — not another living soul. Mom told me so herself.

We were all alone, the three of us, in the middle of a wilderness. Surrounded by alligators and buzzards and snakes.

This was definitely not good!

Plus, there was something spooky about all those jungle plants.

I mean, the sun shone over our clearing, and over the Everglades themselves. But when I walked on the little driveway, the foliage was so dense I couldn't see the sky. No kidding — the trees and bushes actually blotted out all the light!

Just amazing.

Mom tried to get me interested in the plants, of course. She pointed out the Australian pines and all the different kinds of palm trees around: coconut and royal and queen and solitaire and cabbage palms, among others.

She told me that thousands of different kinds of palm trees grow around the world. And she showed me banana plants and banyan trees, and I thought she was going to talk for a week without stopping!

As if I care about any of this. Give me a break!

Don't get me wrong — I like learning about science and stuff in school. And I don't mind admitting that I get pretty good grades on every report card.

But I'm no geek.

I'm interested in the stars and planets and asteroids and things like that. I'd like to be an astronomer when I grow up — and maybe even become an astronaut and fly to Mars, or some other distant world.

That would be the coolest thing I could imagine!

I don't care about plants at all, though. I'm really sick of hearing about them all the time from my mom.

But I was still curious to find out why she brought her lab equipment on our vacation. Finally, as we walked with Timmy among the jungle trees, she told me.

"Well, Jason, I have a theory I want to test," Mom said. "You see all that grass out there in the Everglades? They call it sawgrass because it has sharp edges that can cut you all up. But I think the sawgrass may have something really special about it."

"Really, Mom? What's so special about grass growing in a swamp?" I asked.

"I think that grass might make us a lot of money, Jason. I think sawgrass may contain chemicals that would make it a great fertilizer," Mom explained. "If that's true, I could show farmers how to grow their crops a lot faster than they can now. They could grow more food — and we'd be rich because I could patent the process. No one could use it unless they paid me."

"Wow, it would be awesome to be rich," I said.

"I wanna be wich, too," Timmy babbled.

My brother! He doesn't even know what money is.

"But Mom, I don't get it. Where would you get all this sawgrass for fertilizer?" I wondered.

"Right from here at first, Jason," Mom said. "Maybe later we could find ways to grow it somewhere. But we'd start by harvesting the grass out of the Everglades. We'd bring machines into a place just like this — maybe even right here. And they could scoop up all the grass we would ever need."

"What would happen to the Everglades, Mom? Wouldn't the machines hurt it?" I said.

"Huh? Oh, uh — not much, really," Mom replied. "It's a really, really big place, Jason. This kind of harvesting wouldn't do much damage. Well, maybe some damage, I guess. But this could be an important discovery, son. And remember, it could make us very rich!"

"Cool!" I said.

"Yeah, real cool," Mom said, smiling.

"Yeah, weal cooool," Timmy repeated.

But, even if this vacation might make us rich in the end, I still had nothing to do.

This was only our first afternoon in the hot, humid Florida swamp, and I was already bored stiff.

Mom told me to watch Timmy while she waded into the swamp in rubber wading boots. I saw her sloshing around in the water, pushing an inflated raft with some test tubes and other equipment laid out on it.

"I'm going to make some cuttings of this sawgrass to run the first couple of tests," she yelled. "I just need a few samples to start the experiments."

"Yeah, OK, great, fine," I answered from onshore.

Whatever. All I knew was that I felt incredibly hot, and I wanted to go home.

The water seemed to be flowing around Mom as she stood surrounded by the tall grass, cutting off pieces that she dropped into the glass tubes.

Then I saw something terrifying: two, beady

black eyes rising out of the swamp.

Surfacing behind the sinister eyes was a long dark head. And then an even longer dark body. And then a still longer black tail.

It was an alligator — an enormous, hungry gator just five feet away from my mother!

It was moving toward her, fast!

"Mom! Run!" I screamed. "*Gator!*"

But it was too late for her to run.

The alligator was only a foot from Mom's legs. In another instant, she was going to be chomped to bits!

Chapter Three

The alligator slithered rapidly through the swamp grass, ready to strike.

"Mom, lookout!" I bellowed, pointing at the gator.

Timmy didn't know what was happening — except that I was really upset. He started screaming and crying, too.

Tannin began to bark his head off.

Mom looked startled, not sure where to look or what to do. Then she saw the alligator. Her uncertainty turned to panic.

I saw her eyes open wide with fright as she struggled to move away from the gator attack in time.

"Ahhhh!" she shouted, trying desperately to run through the water.

But the alligator was already upon her.

It rammed her with its stubby nose — and then it did something really strange for a killer reptile.

It just bounced off her.

The gator only thumped into my mother's leg and then continued floating on by.

Mom burst out laughing!

"Ha, ha, ha, ha! I don't believe it!" she cackled. "Oh, that's just too funny!"

"Mom, are you losing it in the heat or something?" I hollered to her. "Get out of that water! You almost got eaten by an alligator. He might come back!"

"Ha, ha, ha, ha! That's no alligator, Jason. Ha, ha, ha!" Mom answered, laughing uncontrollably. "Ha, ha, ha, ha! It was nothing but an old log floating through the water! Ha, ha, ha, ha, ha!"

"You're kidding," I said. "It looked just like an alligator."

"It fooled me, too!" Mom said, still laughing. "It looked just the same shape and color as a gator in the water. But the eyes were only two knots in the log — and the tail was a long branch still attached to the stump. Ha, ha, ha!"

I was glad *she* thought it was so funny. I didn't.

I had been sure I was about to watch my own mother swallowed for lunch by some slimy beast. I was still in shock.

Mom waded slowly back to shore, pushing her sawgrass samples on her inflatable raft. She explained that alligators aren't really the people-eaters most of us think.

"Yes, gators can be dangerous, Jason," she said. "That's why I got so frightened at first. But they don't usually attack grown-ups unless they're provoked or guarding their young or something of that sort. They're really more interested in just going their own way through the Everglades. They don't normally bother anyone."

"So I don't have to worry if I see an alligator, Mom?" I asked. "It won't hurt me?"

"No, that's not true, Jason. You need to be very careful," she answered. "Hungry alligators have been known to attack children — especially small ones, like Timmy. And they'll go after pets, too. So keep an eye on Tannin."

Great. So now I didn't have to be afraid of my mother getting eaten by an alligator. Just Tannin or Timmy.

Or me!

And, of course, I still had to worry about buzzards and snakes everywhere.

As the afternoon sun poured down on us, I began to feel like it was up to me to protect my whole family. I was the oldest boy, after all. And Mom was too busy working on her experiments to guard against any animal attacks.

I felt like a great hunter leading an expedition to the interior of a vast, threatening wilderness. It was my job to bring everyone back alive.

But the great hunter was wilting under the terrible heat.

I have never felt sunshine so blistering or humidity so suffocating. It seemed like I couldn't draw a breath, like the air was as thick as chocolate pudding.

The ground gave off great waves of heat that

shimmered from the shoreline and blended with the horizon. It was hard to tell where the water ended and the air began.

Of course, the great hunter stood guard anyway — watching Tannin, keeping track of Timmy.

And looking after Mom, too! What if that log *had* been an alligator?

I sensed there was serious danger in the Everglades. Horrible, life-threatening danger.

A danger that might destroy our whole family.

And I was right.

But I didn't know this danger would come from something more deadly than any alligator could ever be!

Chapter Four

The first night in the huge Florida swamp was creepy.

I've never heard so many strange sounds — bizarre screeches and spooky howls and weird cries!

I jumped each time we heard something. Timmy was too tired to care. He was already falling asleep, even though it was only 9 o'clock.

Even Tannin's barking didn't keep my little brother awake.

"Shhh! Tannin, stop it!" my mom kept telling the beagle. "It's just some owls or something. Now stop barking, boy."

We all sat together in the living room. Mom read to me from a poetry book. The three of us huddled together on the couch as the single kerosene lamp threw weird, heavy shadows on the cabin walls.

It was still incredibly hot, inside and outside. We were all sweating and wiping our foreheads.

"Mom, I like poetry and everything. But it's hard to concentrate with all these scary noises outside," I complained.

"Jason, now listen to me — there's nothing to be afraid of out here. We're all alone, miles from civilization," Mom responded.

"Yeah, that's why I'm scared," I said. "We're in the middle of a place where human beings don't belong. Anything could come after us in the night: alligators or buzzards or snakes. There are probably spiders around here, too. And other nasty things that don't like people."

"Nonsense! I feel perfectly at home out here," Mom said. "And if there are spiders and other nasty things, they won't hurt you in this cabin. We're completely safe. Now may I keep reading, please?"

"Sure, Mom," I said.

I felt a little ashamed for being so frightened. I am twelve and a half, after all.

"OK, so I'm going to read another poem now, all right? It's a short one by William Blake, who lived in the late 1700s," she told me. "The poem is called 'The Garden of Love,' and it goes like this:

'I went to the Garden of Love
And saw what I never had seen:
A Chapel was built in the midst,
Where I used to play on the green ... ' "

But Mom never got to finish the poem. Because just when she said the word "green," something thumped against the roof of our cabin.

It was a sudden, hard banging on the old tin roof, very loud and very determined. As though a heavy animal had climbed to the top of the cabin to claw its way inside!

Paaaaakk! Paaaaakk! Paaaaakk! Paaaaakk!

"Mom, what's th-that?" I nearly shouted. I moved closer to her on the couch.

I could tell she was scared, too, though she was trying not to show it.

"Uh, I — I don't really, uh, know, Jason," she said. "Probably nothing."

"Nothing? Listen to it, Mom! Something really strong is pounding against our roof!" I said. "It's coming in after us!"

The banging grew louder.

Timmy woke up from the crashing sounds, and started crying. Tannin was barking, his face turned up toward the roof.

"Timmy, don't cry. It's all right. Jason, just calm down. And Tannin, stop that barking!" Mom said. "Probably some animal got up there by accident and is trying to find its way down now. It's just as scared as we are. I'll get a flashlight and go outside to look."

"Outside? Mom, you can't go outside. It's dangerous out there," I said. "The animal might attack you!"

The battering against the tin roof continued: *Paaaaaakk! Paaaaaakk! Paaaaaakk! Paaaaaakk!*

"You're being silly, Jason," Mom said nervously, as she reached for the flashlight. She walked slowly toward the door. "I'll just go, uh, take a quick look. I'll be fine."

"Well, then I'm coming with you! I've got to

help protect this family. I can't let you go alone," I insisted. "Wait for me!"

"Fine, then. We'll both take a look. There's probably something interesting to see up there anyway," Mom said. She opened the door a crack.

Scientists sometimes call the strangest things "interesting!"

This didn't seem interesting at all. It seemed terrifying!

"Just wait right there, Timmy. We'll be right back. And stop barking, Tannin!" Mom ordered.

Very slowly, Mom and I stepped out onto the porch and closed the door behind us. The flashlight beam cut a narrow hole through the blackness, allowing us to see only little patches of things.

First, a small patch of wooden porch. Then, a small patch of dusty ground. Then, a small patch of dirty cabin walls.

And, finally, a small patch of the shiny roof.

The animal would soon come into view, I thought. It was probably some vicious swamp cat clawing at the cabin. Or maybe a huge swamp bird hacking through the hot tin.

When the flashlight reflected off the metal roof, though, the pounding abruptly stopped.

We saw absolutely nothing!

No swamp cats. No swamp birds. Nothing at all!

All was silent, except for the croaking of frogs in the great swamp.

All was dark, except for the thin flashlight beam drifting up toward the pale stars, and into the branches over the cabin roof.

There were dozens of them hanging low over the roof, looking dark and thick and somehow menacing in the night.

Chapter Five

My mother looked at me but said nothing.

We walked back inside the cabin without a word. Mom guided us with the beam of light. I thought I saw her hand shake a little as she turned the flashlight off.

She calmed Timmy by giving him a glass of milk from our tiny refrigerator. Really, the fridge was an old icebox, just a chest that keeps things cold with a block of ice.

Then she filled Tannin's water bowl for the night. It was so hot inside the cabin that our poor little beagle was panting all the time, lapping up water every few minutes.

But Mom knew I was too old to be comforted by a bedtime drink. So she didn't even ask if I was thirsty. Instead she tucked Timmy into the bottom bunk for the night, then sat down on the couch to talk with me.

"I can tell you're worried about something, Jason. What's bothering you?" she asked.

"Mom, I don't understand what happened on the roof. What could have made that awful noise? There was nothing up there at all," I said.

"It had to be some kind of animal, Jason. It was probably a panther or wild cat. When we were shining the light around, it escaped into the trees. Those cats are afraid of people. That's all it was," she answered.

"I don't think so, Mom," I said. "We'd have heard a cat trying to get away. It had to be something else."

"Something else? Like what, for instance?" Mom said.

"Like, well . . . Well, like maybe . . . I *don't know* what!" I said. "But there's something spooky about this place, Mom. I don't like it. Can't you get your samples of grass and then let us get out of here? We could still stop in Orlando for a few days."

"Nice try, Jason," Mom said, smiling. "I

know you'd rather be someplace else for our Florida vacation. But I think you're going to find the Everglades will grow on you. It's a wild, beautiful environment. You'll see. This will be a really memorable vacation, after all."

"I think it will be a really *weird* vacation, after all!" I said. "No theme parks. No beaches. No girls. And no *fun*!"

"Remember, Jason, I'm doing research that may bring our family a great deal of money," Mom pointed out. "If we become rich off the Everglades sawgrass, you'll be able to go to many theme parks and beaches — and meet many, many girls."

"Hmmmm," I said, smiling. "You may have a point."

"Honestly, Jason," she said. "That was just some old cat that climbed on our roof by accident. I'm sure it won't happen again. There's nothing to be afraid of here. Tomorrow, I plan to spend most of the day in the field doing research. But after that, I should have lots of time to spend with you and Timmy."

"Really?" I asked.

"Absolutely. I'm renting an airboat for the rest of the week. We'll be able to go into the Everglades and look for alligators and all kinds of animals."

"Really? You're renting a boat for us? That's way cool," I said. I thought I might have some fun in that big swamp, after all.

"Not just a boat. An *airboat*," Mom said. "It has a big fan in the back, like an airplane propeller, and the boat rides on air so that we can skim over the grass and rocks in the Everglades."

"Awesome!" I said. "Can I drive it?"

"Well, we'll see about that. *Maybe*. But I want you to get to bed now, all right? We all need to get some sleep because we'll wake up at dawn out here," Mom said. "Good night, Jason. I love you. Don't worry about anything. We're perfectly safe in our cabin."

"Good night, Mom. I love you, too," I said, kissing her cheek.

I admire my mother a lot. She always tries to act strong and courageous, no matter what happens. Even when she's feeling scared.

I could tell she was nervous when we were outside looking for whatever was pounding our roof. And when we found nothing there, she was scared for a while. She knew something was strange.

But Mom always finds some logical explanation for everything and then she feels better. I wish I could do that.

I didn't completely believe the loud noises came from a cat on our hot tin roof, but I tried to forget my fears. The sweltering heat was making me tired, anyway.

I brushed my teeth and touched my lucky stone on the dresser, just to be safe. I wanted all the luck I could get in the Everglades.

I climbed into the top bunk, above Timmy. It seemed even hotter up there, but I soon fell asleep, listening to the croaking of frogs and the strange, distant cries of wild creatures.

Maybe it was birds, maybe cats, maybe alligators. I didn't know what was making the faraway sounds — and right then, I didn't want to know. I wanted to dream about pleasant things and hope for the best.

I felt relieved when I awoke in the morning, with bright, cheerful sunshine streaming in our bedroom window. Everything seemed fine.

I could hear Mom making breakfast in the kitchen. Tannin barked softly once or twice.

I looked over the side of my bed and found Timmy was still asleep. And nothing had disturbed *me* during the night.

Our whole family was safe.

Then I looked at the dresser in our room. What I saw made me shiver despite the morning heat.

A trail of green slime was smeared across the dresser, gross and gooey like glue. It dripped off the furniture on to the floor, making a sticky green puddle of gunk.

Something disgusting had climbed through the window at night, leaving the trail of slime. And taking with it the only possession I really cared about.

My lucky stone was gone, stolen by the creature from the green lagoon!

Chapter Six

"Tannin, stay away from that slime!" I shouted.

He was barking, snarling, sniffing the goo, and acting angry that it had invaded the cabin.

I had called Mom when I first spotted the green slime, yelling to her from the bedroom and waking up Timmy. When she ran to me, Tannin followed.

Now the small bedroom was in chaos.

Mom was trying to examine the gunk, but she had to hold back Tannin and answer Timmy's questions at the same time.

"Mommy, what's wrong?" Timmy asked, looking nervously at the slime. "What *is* that, Mommy?"

"I don't know yet, honey," Mom said. "I'm

trying to find out. Tannin, be quiet!" She struggled to hold onto the dog's collar.

"Mom, that's the grossest stuff I've ever seen," I said. "What was in here last night?"

"If Tannin would just cooperate a little, maybe I could tell you," Mom groaned. "Tannin, stop barking! Jason, will you help me, please?"

I took Tannin by the collar and pulled him to the living room. I left him there and ran back into the bedroom, closing the door behind me. I could still hear Tannin growling and scratching at the door.

"Mom, what kind of thing could leave a trail of green goo like that?" I asked. "It's so weird!"

"Mommy, what that?" Timmy babbled.

Our mother bent over the dresser and inspected the slime carefully. She even smelled it two or three times. Then she reached out and touched it!

"Oh, *grosssss*!" I said. "Mom, don't touch it! You don't know what it might be."

Timmy made a twisted face, too.

"Icky!" he said.

"I'm not sure what it is. Not positive anyway," Mom said thoughtfully. She sounded more like a curious scientist now than a mother. "But I'm quite certain it's not dangerous. It's organic. And it didn't come from any animal."

"Didn't come from an animal? How do you know that?" I wondered.

"I can tell from the composition, Jason. It's from some kind of plant. Very interesting, really," Mom responded, examining the goo closely again. "I've never seen anything quite like it. I'll take some samples and bring them back to the lab with me for analysis. In the meantime, I wouldn't worry about it."

"Mom, I've been *slimed*!" I protested. "How can you say not to worry about it? Something came in our bedroom last night through the window, left a bunch of green gunk, and stole my lucky stone!"

"My best theory about what happened, boys, is that a small animal like a raccoon came inside looking for food," Mom explained. "It was probably carrying some kind of plant in its mouth. Or maybe the animal had rolled around in this green substance somewhere outside among all the vegetation. Then the animal brought the substance inside and, for some strange reason, made off with your lucky stone. That part puzzles me a little, I admit."

"Mom, even I know raccoons don't eat stones! And if it was carrying a plant in its mouth when it came in the cabin, how did it carry the stone out without leaving the plant behind?" I replied.

"Good point, Jason. That's very strong, logical thinking. I admit, my theory has some holes," Mom said. "It's hard to explain it better without more information. There might have been two raccoons, for example. Or maybe it wasn't a raccoon. It could have been another type of animal that was attracted to your stone, for some reason. But I do know it's nothing to be concerned about."

"You keep saying that. But I keep feeling pretty concerned anyway," I said.

Mom got one of her lab equipment bags, scooped up several samples of the slime, then cleaned the green, gooey mess the best she could with soap and water. But there was no way to get it all up.

"Stay away from that part of the floor now, boys. It's still very sticky," she warned.

Mom washed and dressed Timmy as I put on my shorts and T-shirt and flip-flops. Then she brought us to the kitchen, keeping the bedroom door shut so Tannin wouldn't end up stuck in the gunk.

After a tasty breakfast of scrambled eggs and bacon and toast, the whole family took a walk together, down the dirt driveway to the narrow paved road leading out of the Everglades. I wished we were in our car headed for Orlando.

Instead, we just strolled down the road for a mile or so. Mom pointed out tropical birds and lizards and plants.

"See that tree, boys? That's a red mangrove tree. Normally you see them along the coast, in salt water. All those curved things that look like sticks around the trunk are really the tree's roots," Mom told us.

"That's nice, Mom," I said politely. Really, I could have cared less.

"And that tree over there is a traveler's palm. It's not really a palm tree but it looks like one," she continued. "It's called a traveler's palm because the stem of each leaf holds about a quart of fresh water,

37

which a thirsty traveler could drink. It's related to the banana trees I showed you yesterday."

"Cool," I said, bored to death.

That is how it went for an hour or so. Mom likes to educate Timmy and me about things — and that's fine, I guess. No one with any sense wants to be stupid all his life.

I don't mind, as long as Mom isn't educating us about plants. But she usually is.

When we finally got back to the cabin, Mom told me I was in charge for the rest of the day. She had to go pick up the airboat — then head into the Everglades all day for her research.

I complained about it. I didn't want her to leave us alone in the middle of a huge swamp.

It was no use. She said I was old enough to take care of my brother and our dog by myself — especially since there were no other people around to bother us.

"Jason, I have to do this work. Remember all the money it might bring us, son. Just give me this one day away. I promise we'll be together the rest of the vacation," Mom said. "And don't forget, I'll have an airboat when I come home tonight. Tomorrow, we can ride in it — all day, if you like."

"OK, Mom. Sure," I said, forcing a smile. "You go ahead. We'll be fine."

Inside, I wasn't so sure.

Timmy and I waved good-bye. Tannin barked and ran alongside the car as Mom drove away. When the station wagon turned the corner and rolled out of sight, I felt very alone.

And very afraid.

I was by myself now, responsible for the safety of a three-year-old brother who could hardly talk and always wanted to "go potty." I had nothing to defend us from danger except my own wits — and a beagle so small he wouldn't frighten a mouse.

Was this a crummy vacation or what?

I didn't know what to do, so I gave Timmy a new coloring book and crayons. He loved to color. Sometimes he played with his crayons for a long time.

Then I pulled out Mom's poetry book and sat on the front porch with Tannin, reading and wiping the sweat from my forehead.

It was blistering hot again — worse than the day before. Some like it hot, but not me.

With the sun climbing higher in the clear, morning sky, I felt the jungle heat wrapping itself around me now, like a woolen blanket in the sauna.

I'd never felt so hot in my life. Tannin panted heavily, often walking slowly inside for a drink of water. Timmy didn't seem to care about the heat, though.

He was too busy coloring. Such a goofy little kid!

I sat there, reading poetry by people like William Blake and Robert Frost and Edgar Allan Poe. Some of it is pretty cool, really.

I lost myself in the beautiful words and pretty soon I wasn't feeling so afraid anymore.

Until I heard the footsteps.

Krroook! Krroook! Krroook!

Through the jungle behind the cabin, they came closer and closer.

Krrrooook! Krrrooook! Krrrooook!

Closer and closer!

Krrrrooook! Krrrrooook! Krrrrooook!

My heart pounded furiously. The hair on my neck stood up straight. I felt dizzy from fear.

We were twenty miles from any living human being!

Who could it be? *What* could it be?

Krrrroooook! Krrrroooook! Krrrroooook!

I was terrified!

Suddenly, a fat, hairy, ugly face poked around the corner of the cabin!

The man wore a patch over his right eye. His two front teeth were missing, and he had long gray hair and a thick, filthy beard.

He smiled wickedly, looking me over as though I were a Thanksgiving turkey in a supermarket.

"Got any children here I can *eat*?" he growled.

Chapter Seven

Before I could think, I screamed!

I jumped up and raced behind Tannin, who was barking loudly at the old man.

What should I do? My mind raced.

Should I dash inside the cabin and lock the door? No, the door had no lock!

Should I grab Timmy's hand and make a run for it? No, Timmy couldn't run very far — and I probably couldn't carry him for long!

Should I tell the old man that I wouldn't taste very good for breakfast? No, he looked *hungry*!

The old man's gap-toothed grin grew wider.

"Take it easy, sonny," he said. "I ain't eaten a little boy for at least a good three years or more! 'Sides, you're too scrawny to make a real meal anyhow."

Then he laughed — a full, rough, powerful laugh, as if he'd just heard the world's funniest joke.

"And you, doggy. Just quiet down there, boy," the old man said, holding out his hand to Tannin.

Tannin sniffed the fat, dirty hand and stopped barking.

"That's it, boy," the man said. "I ain't gonna hurt you."

"What, uh, what do you want, mister?" I asked nervously. I tried to think of a good lie to tell him, something that would make him leave us alone.

"My mom's going to be right back with the police. We had some trouble out here last night. Maybe the policemen can help you. They should all be back here in a couple minutes."

"Oh, so your mom went after the police, eh?" the old man said, grinning. "Well, she's gonna have to drive a long way, she is. There ain't no police around for fifty miles. But listen, sonny. Don't be scared of me. Honest. I ain't gonna hurt nobody."

"Who are you, anyway? And what are you

doing way out here in the Everglades?" I demanded.

"Ah, so *you're* asking the questions, eh? Well, that's OK, I guess. I'm at your cabin, ain't I?" the old man said. "My name's Snake-eye. That's 'cause I've only got this one good eye here. Looks kinda like a snake's eye, don't it? My right eye got ate by a gator."

"A gator!" I shouted. "An alligator ate your eye?"

"Yep. Took it clean out. It's a long story, sonny. Maybe I'll tell you sometime," Snake-eye said. "I live right here in the 'Glades. This is my home."

I scratched my head. I guess I must have looked confused.

"The 'Glades, sonny!" he said. "The Everglades is my home. Ten years ago, I built myself a little cabin right around that bend over there."

Snake-eye pointed to part of the shoreline maybe a half-mile away.

"Last night, I noticed there was people staying in the ol' cabin here. So I just come up to say howdy and see who's visiting. That's all. Just being friendly."

"Why would anyone want to live out *here*?" I asked. "It's hot and infested with alligators and buzzards and snakes. It's a terrible place," I said.

"Nah, sonny, it's a *great* place!" he said. "You just gotta get to know it some first. The 'Glades is like nowhere else on this whole earth of ours. I think it's the most beautiful spot anywhere — as long as people don't come out here and try to mess things up."

"How could anyone mess things up?" I asked.

I thought about Mom's experiments. I hoped Snake-eye hadn't been sneaking around our cabin, listening to her plans for cutting sawgrass from the Everglades.

"People are *always* trying to mess up the 'Glades, sonny. But no matter how hard they try, the 'Glades always finds a way to survive. Yep, she always fights back, she does."

He laughed gruffly.

"See, I come out here 'cause I was tired of people's ways. I don't like the way people only care

45

about money and nothing else matters. They'd ruin the 'Glades and anything else in nature, if it would make them rich enough."

I gulped. Maybe he *had* heard Mom talking about the sawgrass. Maybe he wanted to stop us from getting rich off the Everglades, no matter what he had to do.

"Yep, sonny. I swear if I knew somebody was gonna hurt this ol' swamp, I don't know what I'd do to them," Snake-eye said. "I'm afraid to think about how mean and nasty I might get."

"You'd get, uh, *nasty*?" I asked, my voice quavering.

"You bet I'd get nasty to people like that, sonny! I'd get nasty as a gator with a bellyache, I would," Snake-eye snarled.

He stared down at me angrily. His voice got louder now. He was almost bellowing.

"Why I'd probably just take out my little hatchet and cut people like that down to size, yessir! I'd probably cut them up into little pieces — and use them for fishing bait instead of worms!"

Snake-eye reached down and touched

something hanging from his old leather belt.

It was a hatchet, the clean, steel blade gleaming in the Florida sun!

A hatchet big enough and heavy enough and sharp enough to turn Timmy and me both into fish food.

Chapter Eight

Snake-eye pulled the hatchet from his belt and ran his thumb over the blade.

"I take good care of this ol' hatchet of mine. Never know when I'll need her," he said softly, his left eye glaring at me.

"I h-h-hope you, uh, won't need her around h-here," I answered. I felt frozen with fright.

"Around *here*? At this ol' cabin of yours? Nah, sonny!" Snake-eye said with a deep laugh. "Ain't no one around here I'm aiming to cut up for bait."

He slid the hatchet back into his belt, so the handle hung along his hip.

"You worry too much, boy! A kid your age should be out having fun, chasing frogs and climbing trees and catching fish. You wouldn't feel so nervous. It's too nice a day to sit in the shade reading. Get out in the sunshine, sonny!"

"I don't want to do anything except go home! I don't see how you can stand to live here anyway. I hate it," I said.

"Like I told you, I got tired of people's ways. I love it out here in the open air. I used to live in a crowded ol' apartment building in Fort Lauderdale. Too many people. I can't give my best unless I've got room to move," he said.

"There's plenty of room out here, all right. But what did you do in Fort Lauderdale?" I asked. "You must have had some kind of job if you paid for an apartment."

"I was a fishing boat captain," Snake-eye replied. "I took rich people out in the ocean to catch fish. But one day, I just had enough. And I quit. I don't miss the rich people one bit, I can tell you. But I miss the sea sometimes. I started fishing in the Atlantic Ocean when I was your age — and I went out after fish almost every day for 40 years."

He was talking quietly now, smiling at his memories. But I still didn't trust this old man of the sea.

He could be crazy, I thought. Or some kind of wild kid-killer.

He could be anything.

And I was supposed to protect Timmy all day long while Mom was gone.

I glanced inside the cabin and saw that my little brother was still busy with his coloring book. Maybe Snake-eye didn't even know Timmy was there.

I decided I had to try to get rid of the old man.

"It's nice of you to stop by like this, Mr. Snake-eye," I said. "But I . . . "

"Just Snake-eye, sonny. No 'mister,' " he interrupted. "No one's called me 'mister' since I come out to the 'Glades. I want to keep it like that."

"Sorry. But listen, uh, Snake-eye. I have some chores to do before Mom comes back. She won't be gone long," I lied. "I think you'd better go now. But thanks for coming to visit us."

"So your mom will be home soon, eh? Hmmm. Well maybe she will and maybe she won't,"

Snake-eye said. "But I just come over to be friendly, sonny. Seems like you're trying to get rid of me. And I was just getting comfortable here."

Uh-oh, I thought. Snake-eye *won't* leave.

"No, I'm not trying to get rid of you, Snake-eye. Not at all," I lied again. "But I really do have some chores. And besides, I'm feeling kind of, uh, sick from the heat. I have a headache and everything, you know? I should probably go inside and lie down."

"Well, maybe I can give you something to make you feel better," Snake-eye persisted. "I carry a little bag of herbs from the 'Glades that's good for all kind of ailments. I'll stay and make sure you're all right."

"No! Thanks. That's nice of you. But I'll just go lie down inside for a while," I said. "You can go. I don't want to keep you from fishing or whatever you need to do. I'll be fine."

"Now, sonny, you ain't being real neighborly to an ol' fella that don't get to talk to other folks much," Snake-eye said, grinning at me. "I ain't sure I'm really wanting to move along just yet."

"*Please*, Snake-eye! We can talk again another time. I promise! We'll be here all week," I pleaded.

I waited for his answer, praying he'd leave us alone.

"Well all right, sonny," he said, shrugging his shoulders. "I don't want to stay where I ain't wanted. You sure are a funny kid. You should stop worrying so much. Just be careful out here in the 'Glades, boy! It can be a dangerous place. If you need help, my cabin's right over there, not too far away. You just come and get me, you hear?"

"Yes, sir. Thanks, Snake-eye," I said, moving toward the front door. I was positive I wouldn't want his help, ever. "Have a nice day!"

Snake-eye let out one of his rough, loud belly-laughs. He shook his head and slowly walked away.

I heard footsteps leaving our cabin.

Whew, I thought. What a creepy guy!

I was glad he was gone.

Then I noticed something else seemed to be gone, too. I couldn't see Tannin!

"Here, boy! Tannin!" I called from the porch. "Come on, Tannin! *Taaaanin!*"

He was nowhere in sight.

I took Timmy by the hand and walked around the cabin, inside and out.

I whistled for our little beagle. I hooted for him. Both Timmy and I called out his name.

"Taaaana," Timmy said, which was the best he could do.

"*Taaaanin!*" I shouted.

There was still no sign of the dog.

This wasn't like Tannin at all. He never strayed far from the family. Even when he did, he always barked and ran home when we called.

I was getting frantic.

Mom was not around to help. And I knew something must have happened to our pretty golden beagle.

Tannin had simply disappeared — vanished without a trace into the vast, forbidding Everglades!

Chapter Nine

Timmy started to cry.

"Tanna! I want Tanna! Mommy, Mommy," he whined.

I knew Timmy understood that I was afraid, so I tried to calm myself down. Then I reassured him softly.

"It's all right, Timmy," I said. "We'll find Tannin. He's just out chasing frogs or something. Mommy's not here right now, but she'll be back later. Come on, let's go find Tannin."

Holding hands, we walked down the dirt driveway calling our beagle's name.

No reply.

We even checked out along the paved road for several hundred yards.

Still no Tannin.

Back at the cabin, we both yelled and yelled.

"*Taaaanin!*" I shouted.

"*Taaaanaa!*" Timmy hollered.

There was only one place left to look, though I dreaded the thought of going there. But I knew I had no choice.

I would have to venture into the jungle, into the thick tropical forest of trees and shrubs and vines at the edge of the Everglades. Tannin must have wandered into the woods and become lost.

If I didn't go find him, he might never come home.

I took Timmy back inside the cabin, after he stopped briefly at the outhouse. At least he didn't have an accident. That's always so gross!

I gave him two more coloring books. I hoped they would keep him busy long enough for me to find Tannin.

"You stay right there, Timmy!" I ordered. "Do you understand? No matter what happens, you wait right in this cabin for me or Mom to come back."

Then I walked toward the jungle. My legs

shook, I was so scared.

There was no path through this forest of tall, leafy trees and long, thick vines and round, prickly bushes. It was just a huge mass of green that spread out for miles and miles.

The heat was worse than ever now. The humidity seemed so high, the air seemed so damp, that it was hard to draw a full breath.

Turkey buzzards filled the sky, circling under the fierce sun.

I knew that I might stumble over all kinds of terrible creatures in the tropical forest: snakes and panthers and lizards.

I tried one last time to call for Tannin, desperately hoping he would come running out of the trees wagging his tail.

"*Taaaaaaaaaanin!*" I screamed.

Still nothing. No barking. No wagging tail.

So I entered the jungle, step by careful step, determined to rescue our beloved beagle.

I had no idea where I was going, I wasn't sure I could find the way back. What if I got lost, too? What if I walked so deep into the jungle that I never found my way out?

The jungle forest was dark and getting darker the deeper into it I walked. Only a few rays of sunshine poked through the heavy growth of green.

I had to push the broad leaves of palmetto and elephant ear plants out of my path, just to inch forward. Mosquitoes and flies and gnats buzzed around my head. Sweat poured off my brow.

"*Taaaanin!*" I kept calling. "*Taaaaaaaanin!*"

I brushed past a brown vine hanging from a tall banyan tree — and saw something that sent a chill up my back.

Tannin's collar!

It hung at the bottom of the vine, as if someone had tied the collar to the tree.

The vine was wound tightly around the small, red leather collar — so tightly that I had to rip it loose.

Now I was terrified!

I began to run blindly through the dense jungle, deeper and deeper and deeper into the darkness.

I had to find Tannin! Something had happened to him!

I had to find Tannin *right now!*

I ran so long and so hard through the heat that I was panting just like our dog, struggling for air.

Finally, I had to stop and rest, putting my hands on my knees. My lungs puffed madly for breath.

I raised my head at last and wiped my brow and was about to begin running again, when I saw it.

The saddest sight of my life.

Tannin lay at the bottom of a thick tree, motionless.

"*Tannin!*" I screamed.

He didn't move.

His eyes were closed. I could tell he wasn't breathing.

He just lay on his side, still as a jungle log.

Something — or some*one* — had killed Tannin!

Chapter Ten

I pushed past the leaves and vines, running to Tannin.

"Come on, boy!" I shouted, shaking his little golden body. "Come on, Tannin! You'll be OK!"

I shook him over and over. Tannin was completely limp.

Nothing would ever change that now. Our family pet had been murdered in the Everglades.

I began to cry, brushing away the tears and sweat that washed together over my cheeks.

How had this happened, I wondered. What would have hurt poor Tannin out here in the forest?

Or *who* would have hurt him? I just could not understand what had happened.

I tried to stop crying. What would Mom do in this situation, I asked myself. She'd say it was important to get more information. I had to think like a scientist now, coolly and logically.

So I examined Tannin's body. I found very little at first.

Nothing in his mouth. Nothing in his nose. Just a few shreds of green leaves around his ears.

Then I saw the murder weapon!

It was like no murder weapon I had ever seen on TV detective shows. It was nothing but a long green leaf from a palm tree — a palm *frond*, as Mom would call it.

It lay underneath Tannin, twisted and broken. The stem was curled, as though it had been wrapped around Tannin's neck.

Somebody had torn a palm frond off a tree and strangled our dog!

I quickly realized there was no one out in this thick jungle to do such an awful thing — except for Snake-eye!

He really *was* a crazy killer! He wanted to knock us all off, one by one, so that Mom's research wouldn't harm his precious 'Glades.

Then I remembered something horrifying:

Timmy was back in the cabin at that very moment.

Alone.

A perfect target for Snake-eye!

Tears still dripping down my cheeks, I walked sadly away from Tannin. I knew it was a lot more important to worry about my little brother.

I turned to run toward the cabin to get Timmy out before Snake-eye arrived — but then I stopped.

No, *that* wasn't the right way back.

I turned again and peered through the tangle of dense green trees and bushes and vines, taking several quick steps toward the cabin.

Then I stopped again.

No, *that* wasn't the right way, either.

I looked for bent branches or broken twigs or footprints — any sign that showed me the way I had hurried through the jungle.

I turned. Then I turned again. And then I turned some more and turned one more time and turned just once more and turned around and around and around in circles.

Every direction looked the same. Just green

trees and green bushes and brown vines, on and on and on, everywhere I looked.

I was lost.

Totally and hopelessly lost.

With a mad killer on the loose, a wild man named Snake-eye who was probably near the cabin, stalking closer and closer to my brother.

Or maybe Snake-eye was still in the jungle, nearby, stalking closer and closer to me.

Chapter Eleven

I wanted to cry, but there was no time for that now.

I felt sure that either Timmy was in terrible danger from Snake-eye — or I was!

I had to find a way back to the cabin — *fast!* But I had absolutely no clue which direction to start running.

It was dark in the jungle. Tiny rays of sunshine trickled through the leaves. It was so dim and so hot that I felt as if I'd stepped into an enormous green oven. I was being baked like a loaf of bread.

Jungle birds squawked from the branches. Jungle insects chirped from the bushes. Jungle animals howled in the distance.

Jungle lizards climbed the vines. Jungle monkeys jumped from limb to limb.

I heard a sudden crack in the woods — as if someone heavy had stepped on a tree branch on the ground.

I strained my eyes, peering through the dense tangle. I saw nothing and no one.

I glanced toward Tannin again, then plunged boldly forward through the forest.

The problem was, I still wasn't sure if I was plunging forward or backward or sideways.

I only knew I had to start walking. All I could do was hope I was walking in the right direction.

After a few minutes, though, it got harder and harder to move in any direction. The jumble of leaves and prickly bushes seemed to grow thicker ahead of me.

I pushed more branches and more limbs out of my way with each step I took. But by the time I decided to turn back, the jungle behind me was just as thick. Soon I didn't know how to get out of the dense undergrowth.

I felt trapped, sealed inside a tomb of green leaves.

And it was so hot — *too* hot! I couldn't get any air into my lungs in this place.

I felt like I was suffocating.

Then I thought I saw the leaves actually move toward me, the branches slowly reaching out to grab me by the neck! The trees were going to strangle me!

I was going to die in the Florida forest, just like Tannin!

I knew I must be losing my mind from the jungle heat. I felt so hopeless and so tired and so hot that I couldn't make myself budge an inch through the wall of green leaves.

Until I heard another branch snap, somewhere to my right.

Maybe there was a clearing in that direction, a place where the undergrowth thinned out! Maybe there was a path to take me back toward the cabin!

It was my only hope. I wrestled with the mass of branches, tearing and ripping them to move toward the clearing. They seemed to fight back, to push against my hands and pull at my arms.

At last, I broke through the tangled leaves

and limbs and vines — and I found there really was a clearing.

I smiled and drew a deep, relieved breath of humid air. And found I was not alone.

Standing there, directly in front of me, stood Snake-eye!

He had a sneer on his lips and his hatchet in the air, aimed at my brains!

The steel blade caught a single ray of sunlight and shone bright amid the dense greenery.

Snake-eye had found his next victim — *me!*

He was about to hack me into little slices of fish bait!

Chapter Twelve

I screamed!

"Aaaaaaaahhh!"

I tried to duck before Snake-eye slammed his hatchet down on my head. But there was no time to move out of his way.

I watched the hatchet slice through the air, its deadly steel blade flying toward me.

And then I watched as the hatchet kept on flying, just missing my ear.

Snake-eye sent the hatchet spinning toward the ground. As he did, he yanked me behind him forcefully.

I looked down and realized that the old man had never aimed the hatchet at me at all. He had aimed at a long, striped snake that had slithered on top of a log near my feet.

His hatchet had cut the snake in half.

"By God, sonny! That was a close one!" he said, puffing to get his breath. "I thought you might be a goner there for a second. That's a coral snake, boy! One of the deadliest there is! You keep your eyes open for them red and yellow stripes on a snake next time, sonny. If you see them, you'd better run through this jungle!"

I was almost speechless. Snake-eye had saved my life. I didn't know what to say to him. But I knew now that he wasn't the crazy man I'd imagined.

"Snake-eye!" I blurted out. "I don't know how to thank you."

"Ahh, weren't nothing, sonny," he said. "I was walking through the woods here and heard someone. Knew it had to be you so I followed you to make sure you was OK," he replied. "You look like you're maybe a tad lost out here, eh?"

"Uh, yeah, I guess I am," I admitted sheepishly. "Is there any way you could help me get back to the cabin?"

"Sure, sonny. Just follow me and I'll take

you back home," Snake-eye said. "Say, kid, you got a name?"

"Jason," I said. "My little brother's name is Timmy."

"You got a little brother? Say, that's nice. I never had no brother," Snake-eye said. "Well, all right, then. Come on and follow close to me, Jason. Don't get more than two steps away from me. This here is the heart of darkness. It's easy to get lost in this jungle out here, sonny. Mind if I still call you 'sonny' sometimes? It's just my way of talking to kids."

"You can call me anything you want, Snake-eye," I said. "As long as you can help me find our cabin again."

As we walked, I told Snake-eye what had happened to Tannin.

He stopped dead in his tracks, turning to glare down at me from his left eye.

"You say you seen a palm frond curled around your little doggy's neck, sonny?" he asked. His voice sounded worried.

"Well, um, yeah, Snake-eye. At least it

69

looked like it had been curled around his neck. Why? What's that mean?" I asked.

"It don't mean nothing good, I can tell you that much, kid," Snake-eye replied.

He looked at the ground for a moment, rubbing his long gray hair and stroking his beard. He even raised the black patch over his right eye and scratched the skin there.

Then he motioned with his head for me to follow again, and walked on through the dense tropical woods.

"Tell me, Snake-eye! What happened to Tannin? What does it mean?" I begged.

"Well, sonny, you see there's a legend around these parts. I've never really given it much heed, mind you. But the Seminole Indians in Florida like to tell the tale about what they call 'procoharim,' " Snake-eye explained. "That means, 'the revenge of the plants.' "

"Revenge of the plants!" I gulped. I moved a step closer to Snake-eye as we walked, surrounded by plants.

"Yep. See, this is how the story goes," he

said. "There was these two young Seminole braves who was sent into the 'Glades in a canoe one day to catch fish for their people. They was carrying these two tree-bark pails to put the fish in, one of 'em kind of a dark shade, and the other one whiter, see? But 'stead of fishing, they went on some wild rampage through the 'Glades. They started slashing through the reeds and sawgrass for no reason at all. Just tearing it up with their tomahawks. Then they canoed to this big island and started hacking down trees and ripping up bushes and carving up everything in sight."

"Why would they do that?" I wondered.

"No one knows. It ain't the Seminole way, that's sure enough. Just plain meanness, I guess. Just like some kids today are mean for no reason," Snake-eye said.

"So these braves start canoeing back to the tribe, see, planning to lie to everyone that they couldn't catch no fish," he continued. "But 'stead of that, their canoe starts sinking — a canoe that's also made out of trees, remember! Gators are all around 'em now and these boys start bailing water out of their canoe like crazy, using them tree-bark pails. Well, one pail just jumps out of the brave's hand and skitters away, turning cartwheels 'cross the water! Then the brave falls out, too, and the gators surround him. The other brave, holding the whiter shade of pail, starts bailing furious-like now. But it's no use. That pail jumps out of his hands and bops him on the head! He falls in the water, too!"

"Wow, so they were eaten by gators, then?" I asked, fascinated by Snake-eye's tale.

"No, them braves was able to swim back to the same island in the 'Glades, though they was feeling kinda seasick by now," Snake-eye continued. "The Seminole legend says that the wooden canoe and the tree-bark pails forced these boys back to the place they just destroyed. And once the braves was back on the island, the few palm trees that was left just reached down and killed those boys, one at a time!"

"The palm trees killed them? Just the trees, all by *themselves*?" I gasped.

"Yep, that's what the legend says, sonny. The bodies of the two braves was found the next day," Snake-eye said. "Each of them Indian boys had one long palm frond curled around his neck — the same palm frond that strangled them to death as revenge!"

Chapter Thirteen

"But I don't understand, Snake-eye! That doesn't make any sense," I protested. "Why would the plants take revenge on Tannin? He didn't hurt anything."

"No telling, sonny. Maybe he was ripping up plants with his paws or chewing things up bad out in the woods. Can't really say 'cause I wasn't there when the tree got him," Snake-eye answered. " 'Course, I still ain't sure I really want to give that ol' Indian legend no heed. I hate to think the trees and bushes out here is alive enough to kill folks! No, I'm just telling you the story 'cause it does seem kinda strange, with the curled palm frond and all."

To call it "kinda *strange*" didn't seem strong enough to me. Kinda *bizarre*, maybe.

Kinda *terrifying*, for sure.

74

As we walked back through the thick jungle toward the cabin, I tried to put the legend of "procoharim" out of my thoughts. It was just a silly old story made up to scare young Seminole braves, I told myself.

"Revenge of the plants," indeed.

But somehow, I couldn't believe it was only a tall tale.

Somehow, I felt the Indian legend told a very disturbing truth.

And that made me *extremely* nervous as we pushed through the deep green forest of plant leaves.

Maybe the plants wanted revenge on me, too.

My arm got caught in a snarled mass of hanging vines as I trudged behind Snake-eye. I felt sure the plants were after me!

I shouted for Snake-eye, frantically trying to free myself from the tangle of thick, rope-like vines.

He turned around and carefully worked my arm loose.

"Relax, sonny! You worry too much!"

Snake-eye said. "Them plants wasn't out to strangle you or nothing. Just watch where you're going next time. You got to keep your eyes open real wide in the jungle, boy!"

After that, I opened my eyes as wide as I could, staring at everything around me and following just one step behind my guide.

Finally, we walked from the dark cover of woods into the sunlight again.

What a wonderful feeling! What an incredible relief!

Even though the humidity and heat were worse than ever, I felt as though I could breathe again. I had survived this untamed forest at the edge of the Everglades.

Once more, Snake-eye had saved my life.

"Well, sonny. Here's your cabin. You OK now?" he asked.

"Yes, Snake-eye, I'm fine now. Thanks very, very much! You really saved me in that jungle," I replied. "Do you want to come by the cabin for a glass of lemonade? We can talk some more if you want to."

"Thanks, sonny. Maybe I'll drop by tomorrow and take you up on that. But I got some fishing to do this afternoon. Probably should head along on my way," Snake-eye said. "You be careful now, though, you hear me? I'm going out in the 'Glades in my canoe. I won't be around to watch over you none this afternoon."

"I'll be careful, believe me, Snake-eye. *Very* careful!" I promised. "Thanks again! For everything!"

I watched the old man walk slowly along the edge of the swamp, his hatchet dangling from his belt. I even waved good-bye to him once, but he didn't see me.

I hurried to the cabin, hoping I would not have to clean up some mess my little brother had made. It had been a long time since Timmy had visited the outhouse — after all, I *had* ordered him to wait for me inside the cabin.

I dreaded taking off his sticky pants. Yuck!

"Timmy, I'm back," I said, bounding up the cabin steps. "Timmy, where are you?"

I looked around the living room. My brother

wasn't there.

Only his crayons and coloring books remained where I had last seen him.

I raced through the cabin, calling his name, looking into every corner of every room. I couldn't find him.

I panicked.

It was bad enough when Tannin had disappeared — but this was a hundred times more frightening.

This was Timmy! This was my kid brother!

I ran everywhere at once. Outside and inside. To the outhouse and back to the bedroom. To the porch and to the edge of the huge swamp.

I screamed for him at the top of my lungs.

"*Tiiiiiimmmy!*" I bellowed.

He was nowhere.

Had he drowned in the Everglades? Had an alligator eaten him? Had he wandered into the jungle after me?

I remembered the fate of Tannin and shuddered.

Not Timmy, too!

I flew back inside the cabin for maybe the tenth time, praying Timmy would somehow be magically waiting for me.

But he wasn't.

Then I looked more carefully at his coloring books and noticed something I hadn't seen before.

It was bright green, and it stuck out from between two pages of the book Timmy had been working on. I spread apart those pages and gasped, horrified beyond all words.

It was part of a tropical tree, the curled tip of a single palm frond!

Chapter Fourteen

I began running.

I didn't know where I was going, what I was running to or from.

I just knew I had to get out of that cabin — and find my little brother!

"*Tiiiimmy! Tiiiimmy! Tiiiimmy!*" I screamed.

I flew wildly to the edge of the jungle, racing beside the dark woods, looking for any sign of him. Then I raced down the dirt driveway, watching for Timmy among the vines and bushes and trees there.

I stretched my neck to the right. I stretched my neck to the left.

"*Tiiiimmy! Tiiiimmy! Tiiiimmy!*" I shouted desperately.

As I ran, I thought I heard a rustling among the leaves to one side.

I stopped in my tracks, then hurried back to peer into the dense forest along the driveway.

There is definitely something moving in that heavy patch of green woods, I thought.

I heard the sound of leaves brushing together: *Shoooshashaa*! *Shoooshashaa*! *Shoooshashaa*!

"Timmy!" I yelled. "Timmy, is that you?"

I could make out only a muffled, whimpering little voice in response. But I knew it was my brother's.

Timmy was trapped in the jungle!

Without another thought, I plunged into the plants — and straight into a thick spider web strung between two palm trees.

"*Aaaaaahhh*!" I hollered, my arms flailing.

I tried to wipe the web from my eyes so that I could see Timmy, but the sticky strands clung to my eyelashes. I couldn't even open my eyes.

Finally, I scraped the spider goo from my eyelids — only to discover a large hairy spider sitting on my left shoulder!

Two of its long, woolly legs were raised. The

spider started climbing toward my face.

I hollered again.

Then, with a hard swipe of my hand, I knocked the spider into the forest.

Timmy's muffled voice still strained to cry out for me, as though someone had a hand over his mouth.

Or, maybe, as if some*thing* was wrapped around his throat!

I struggled to push the huge leaves from my path so I could find Timmy. But the leaves didn't move aside.

Instead, they seemed to push me back, shoving harder and harder each time I tried to break through! It was like trying to shoulder my way down a school hallway filled with bullies!

Again and again, I rammed my body into the green leaves. Again and again, the leaves forced me back.

The plants really *are* alive, I thought. The Indian legend is *true*!

The leaves grabbed me like a dozen hands and shoved. I tore into them furiously, trying to shred the green fiends with my fingers.

I managed to rip a large plant-hand in half. I managed to crash through the bushes toward Timmy.

I could hear that he was calling my name. His words were still muffled.

I had to get to him quickly!

When at last I did find Timmy, all my determination and courage drained out of my body.

The poor, confused, terrified little kid was covered by plants!

Their green arms were moving, wrapping themselves tighter and tighter around his ankles and wrists, around his mouth and eyes, around his chest and waist.

And one long palm frond was bending low and curling itself slowly around his neck!

Chapter Fifteen

I was paralyzed with fear.

The jungle was about to strangle Timmy —
and there was nothing I could do about it.

I had to turn and run as fast as I could. I had
to break out of the deadly forest. I had to save myself!

All these thoughts poured through my brain
at once.

Then I looked at Timmy's face, twisted in
fright as he shouted for help through the killer
leaves. I knew I had to try to rescue my little
brother.

I ran to him and began to fight with the
plants like a madman. Twisting and bending, tearing
and breaking — even ripping through the leaves
with my teeth!

Timmy fought, too. His arms never stopped moving for a moment. They whipped and slapped everything around him, as if he were under attack by a hive of bees.

Together, we battled the jumble of angry, green plants.

Finally, Timmy was able to wriggle free. Just barely.

He slid his ankle from the last plant's grip and then ran faster than I knew he could run. I ran right behind him.

The leaves slashed and snatched at us, trying to snare us as we pushed our way through the jungle toward the driveway. We batted them away and pressed on as quickly as we could.

We escaped from the woods on to the dirt drive — and kept running as fast as our legs would move.

"Run, Timmy! Run!" I shouted. "Keep running, all the way back to the cabin! *Ruuunn!*"

The trees and bushes and vines that lined the driveway began to bend low. Their green branches and brown vines stretched toward our legs.

Even the trunks of the tallest palm trees bent themselves over, trying to snag us as we rushed along.

I hurried ahead and scooped up Timmy in my arms now, then ran down the exact middle of the drive.

It was just wide enough so that none of the plants could quite get a hold on us. But I was still forced to kick and punch away the leaves that reached in too close.

The Florida sunshine beat down on us. Turkey buzzards again circled in the sky.

I was exhausted from running, and my T-shirt and shorts were drenched with sweat.

But I kept going, going, going.

Until I could go no more. Without warning, my tired right foot tripped over my tired left foot!

Timmy and I went sprawling on to the driveway, scraping our faces on the gravel as we fell.

Even worse, we both landed within reach of the killer plants.

In another instant, Timmy and I would both be in their clutches, dragged into the jungle to a horrible, painful, green death!

Chapter Sixteen

I saw the long, green plant arms reaching down to pull me into the forest forever.

Immediately, I rolled to my left through the gravel, just out of their reach.

I scrambled to my feet, ran to Timmy, and tore him loose from the bushes before any branch had time to tighten its grip around him.

I gathered him into my arms and began to run again.

I huffed and puffed, breathing so hard in the thick, damp South Florida air that I was afraid my lungs would burst.

When we were at last safely in the clearing, I set Timmy down, then collapsed to the ground, gasping for breath. I lay there for a few moments, feeling dizzy as I listened to Timmy's soft whimpering.

"Mommy, Mommy, Mommy," he kept repeating.

He was sucking his thumb — something he only did when he was very scared.

As the dizziness slowly left me, I glanced toward the sky and saw the buzzards wheeling and turning directly above us. With their wings spread to catch the wind, the large black birds flew in narrowing circles over our heads, waiting for something to drop dead so they could eat the remains.

I watched them turn, turn, turn. Then I understood what the buzzards had been doing all day — they were waiting for *us* to drop dead!

"Come on, Timmy," I said, rising slowly to my feet. "We've got to get inside away from these trees where we'll be safe."

I took him by the hand and walked him inside. There, on his coloring book, lay the curled tip of the palm frond.

"Timmy, how did you get stuck in all those plants?" I asked him. "Can you tell me what happened?"

Timmy just looked confused.

"Mommy! I want *Mommy!*" he insisted.

"Mommy will be back soon, Timmy. I promise. But you have to tell me what happened to you. It's really, really important," I explained softly. "How did you get outside, all tangled up in those plants? Did you walk outside by yourself?"

Timmy shook his head.

"You didn't? Then what happened? Tell me how the plants got all wrapped around your face and arms like that," I said.

Timmy just shook his head again.

"No? Why not? You don't want to tell me what happened?" I asked gently.

Timmy shook his head once more.

"How come? Are you scared?" I said.

This time, he nodded.

"Well, don't be scared. I'm here with you now and I won't leave you alone again," I promised. "Just please tell me what happened. Please, Timmy!"

"Just pull me away," Timmy babbled. "Just pull me away weal fast!"

"Something pulled you away, Timmy? What

was it? What pulled you away from the cabin?" I persisted.

"Twee!" he answered. "Big twee pull me away!"

A tree! Somehow a palm tree had reached inside our cabin and snagged Timmy!

I figured the palm tree must then have passed him among other trees and vines and bushes into the jungle, just like fans at a baseball game pass a hot dog from row to row.

And, instantly, I understood something else: We had to leave the cabin!

If a tree could reach in to grab him once, it could reach in again to grab us both.

But where could we go? There were trees and other plants *everywhere*!

"Snake-eye!" I almost shouted, snapping my fingers. "We've got to go find Snake-eye! He'll know what to do!"

Timmy was crying and I noticed that his pants were wet. I quickly changed him into a dry pair of shorts, grabbed his hand, and together we marched off toward Snake-eye's cabin. I didn't even think about how gross Timmy's wet pants were.

As we walked along the shoreline, far from the trees that strained to reach us, I finally had a moment to think about the plant attacks.

First, Tannin. Then, Timmy. Then, me.

But why? Why would they want to hurt our family?

By the time we arrived at Snake-eye's run-down shack, I still had no idea why the plants were trying to kill us.

Maybe Snake-eye can figure it out, I thought.

"Snake-eye!" I hollered. "Snake-eye, are you here? It's Jason! We're in big trouble! We need your help!"

Snake-eye did not answer.

Then I remembered what he had told me earlier: He was going out fishing for the day. He would not be around to rescue us from trouble.

I figured the best thing we could do was wait beside the front door for Snake-eye to return.

His shack was a real dump, filthy and falling apart. Next to it, our cabin looked like a Hilton hotel.

But at least all the trees were a few hundred yards away. It seemed like the smartest place to hang out, if we planned on staying alive.

Staying alive was the only thing I could think about. All I wanted for our family out of this vacation was survival. I wanted us to get in our station wagon and drive out of the Everglades and go back to Kansas.

And never see Florida again.

But I suddenly realized that might be too much to ask.

Because I noticed something so incredible, so shocking, so ghastly that at first I couldn't believe it was true.

The trees and the bushes were moving!

Not just reaching and stretching toward us, but actually moving forward, as if they were walking. Whole trees and whole bushes were sliding slowly through the ground toward the shack!

By the time I saw what was happening, they were so close that we had no clear path to escape back toward our own cabin.

There was nowhere to run, nowhere to hide. The plants were closing in around us on every side — *except* behind us! Except for the swamp.

The swamp, I thought. There is no other choice.

We would have to *swim* back to the cabin!

I knew Timmy was already a good swimmer, thanks to Mom's lessons, so I took his hand and hurried down to the water's edge.

I took off my flip-flops and Timmy's tennis shoes. We waded into the Everglades.

"Come on, Timmy! It's all right. Let's go swimming. It'll be fun," I lied in a cheerful voice.

But soon I saw more deadly trouble waiting for us: alligators!

Two dark green alligators swam toward us, wiggling among the reeds, their reptile eyes glaring at us hungrily.

Killer gators to the west.

Killer plants to the north, south and east.

And, this time, no Snake-eye to save our lives.

"*Help!*" I screamed, hoping someone — a guide, a fisherman, an Indian, *anyone* — might hear me. "Help, I need *somebody*! *Heeeeelllpp!*"

Chapter Seventeen

I shouted so loudly that my throat got sore.

No one came to our rescue.

We were alone — and surrounded by death.

Timmy was confused now. He started to cry. I wanted to cry, too.

I knew there was no time for panic, though. I had to come up with some way to get us out of there before the plant killers advanced all the way to the swamp.

I remembered what Mom had said about alligators. They were dangerous, yes. But they usually didn't eat people.

Then I remembered that they sometimes snack on children — especially smaller ones like my brother.

Still, what choice did we have? Our only

hope to get away was through the swamp.

I put Timmy on my back, piggy-back style. I grabbed a short stick that floated by, handed it to him, and told him to hang on to it.

Slowly and fearfully, I waded into the enormous swamp.

The narrow, menacing eyes of the two gators watched as we began to swim.

And we swam for our lives. I was barely able to keep us both afloat.

"Kick, Timmy!" I yelled. "Kick with your feet, like Mom showed you! And hold on to that stick!"

I sputtered and spit as I struggled to swim through the black water with Timmy on my back. We were only about a hundred yards from a spot on the shore where there were no jungle plants — at least not yet.

If I could just get us there, we could climb out and run for it.

But the gators weren't through with us yet.

Like huge snakes in the grass, they slithered through the reeds toward us, one behind the other.

They came slowly at first, then faster and faster and faster.

Their beady eyes protruded only slightly above the water, keeping their prey in sight as they prepared to attack.

But we weren't as defenseless as we seemed.

"Timmy, give me the stick," I hollered, taking it from his hand. "Now swim, Timmy! Swim as fast as you can!"

I gave my kid brother a hard push through the water, sending him forward with a splash. Then I turned to face my enemies, treading water with one hand, ready to battle them with the other.

One alligator veered off toward Timmy.

I reached out and bashed him on the snout with the stick and the gator turned sharply — toward me.

He lunged through the water, his mouth open. I smashed him hard on the snout again, then poked him right in the eye.

The gator reeled in pain, and then swam away through the swamp.

The other alligator was closing in on me

now.

Moving swiftly, his powerful tail splashing behind him, the gator charged me.

I waited and waited and waited as the gator eyes grew larger and larger.

When the alligator dove under the water and opened his mouth to bite me, I rammed the whole stick down his throat. It stuck there, hanging out over his sharp, vicious teeth.

The gator howled, thrashing and spinning, full of the sound and the fury of an angry beast. Finally, his jaws clamped down hard, biting the stick in half.

I turned and swam toward the shore as fast as I could. I saw Timmy still paddling through the reeds.

"Swim, Timmy! Swim *faster*!" I bellowed. "Climb up out of the water! Hurry! Hurry!"

I twisted my head and saw that the second alligator had disappeared with the first. Timmy was on shore now, and I wasn't far behind him.

We had made it!

We stretched out on the muddy bank to rest,

dripping and coughing.

"Good boy, Timmy! You did great!" I told him. "You're being such a brave boy! I'm so proud of you!"

"I want Mommy," he complained.

I couldn't blame him. I wanted Mom, too!

I noticed the buzzards circling over our heads again, still looking for dinner. The sun was falling lower in the sky now, round and golden and blistering hot. At least I felt cooler after our gator-infested swim.

"Mommy will be home soon," I said. "Come on, Timmy. Maybe she'll be back by now."

I prayed that I might be right.

I'd never felt so tired in my life. Timmy was totally worn out.

But I forced us to run back to the cabin. The trees and shrubs along the bank snapped and grasped at us all the way.

By now, there was very little room to run between the jungle and the Everglades. The plants on our path also had begun to move, crowding the water line.

100

We had to stay close to the swamp, sometimes splashing along the edge just to keep away from the reaching plants.

I saw our cabin in the distance, and sighed with relief. After fighting off the alligators, I felt confident that I could keep a single palm tree from dragging us into the tropical forest.

And Mom should be back soon anyway, I thought. We'll all jump in the car and leave this awful, dangerous place.

Then I realized something about our cabin looked different.

Very different! *Horribly* different!

The driveway was gone, for one thing, overgrown with the trees and the bushes and the vines! There was no way for Mom to bring the station wagon back and take us away now.

And the cabin's shiny tin roof was completely green, covered in plants!

The jungle was closing in on the cabin, inch by inch, slowly swallowing our vacation home.

I knew that soon the killer jungle would swallow us, too!

Chapter Eighteen

As the tropical forest edged closer and closer, I knew the cabin offered us the only possible protection.

Timmy was too tired to run anymore, so I picked him up in my arms and rushed toward the little wooden shack.

Up the steps and onto the porch I ran, dodging giant leaves and huge branches that stretched out to grab us by the throat.

We were almost inside.

Suddenly, I felt myself jerked backwards. One of the palm fronds had seized Timmy's wrist!

Now I was in a tug-of-war, with the palm tree pulling hard in one direction, and me pulling hard in the other.

And Timmy's arm was the rope!

He started crying as I yanked forcefully to free him.

Timmy moved back and forth, back and forth — to the right a few inches, to the left a few inches.

Finally, the palm frond's grip slipped and Timmy's wrist came loose.

I raced inside with him still in my arms, set him on the floor and slammed the front door. I heard the palm frond banging on the door.

"Mommy! Mommy! I want Mommy!" Timmy bawled.

"I know, Timmy. I know you do. So do I," I answered gently. "But please don't cry now. We have to fight off these plants together and wait for Mom to get back. She'll know what to do."

I heard the plants snaking across the tin roof. The vines squirmed as they grew longer and longer. I heard the tree branches crawling as they reached and strained to climb inside.

Enormous green leaves and brown vines dangled from the roof, twisting and bending in front of our windows like dozens of deadly serpents.

I could see other trees and bushes surrounding the cabin. The entire tropical forest seemed to be rolling through the earth toward our front door. Soon we would be encircled by the jungle.

We were trapped, helpless, and alone.

I heard something crash to the floor in our mother's bedroom. I ran to discover what had happened, leaving Timmy whimpering on the couch.

When I got to her room, I saw that our troubles were quickly growing worse.

The plants already had found their way into the cabin!

The thin bough of an Australian pine tree had poked in through the window, knocking a clay candleholder off the nightstand. The branch was moving toward the living room, coming after us.

I ran to the window and hurled it down on top of the branch, cutting the bough off as though I'd chopped it with an ax.

The stump of the branch banged against the window, but seemed unable to break through the glass.

I remembered we had other windows in the

cabin, though — other entrances for the plants.

I tore into the living room, where Timmy sat curled up on the couch. I closed both windows there before the vines had time to slither inside.

With all the windows shut, the cabin was as hot as a furnace. But our only hope was to suffer through the exhausting heat — and pray the rickety wood cabin and the thick panes of glass would hold back the jungle's fierce assault.

For the moment, we seemed safe enough. I paused to catch my breath.

Suddenly, I heard a loud *boom!* from the back of the cabin, as if something large had dropped onto the floor.

With horror, I remembered the *other* bedroom window. I hadn't closed the window in the room I shared with Timmy!

"Stay here, Timmy! Don't move, all right? Stay right on the couch!" I ordered him.

I ran into our bedroom — and found three broad palm fronds inside.

They were enormous. And they were growing longer and wider as I watched, expanding by maybe an inch every second.

They had rammed into the dresser, dumping it on to the floor. Now they were reaching toward me, like three claws of some green monster.

Should I fight back — or close the bedroom door and run? To flee or not to flee, that was the question!

I knew the claws would soon grow large enough to break through the flimsy bedroom door. If they became that big, Timmy and I would be finished.

I had to kill them now!

I ran around my bed, hoping to sneak up behind the fronds before they could turn to grab me. Then I would slam the window shut. Maybe I could chop them off at the windowsill, just like the pine bough.

As I hurried near the window, though, my foot stuck to the floor! My left foot!

I couldn't move!

I had stepped into the remnants of the green goo, the gunk that had dripped from my dresser during the night.

It was just like glue.

I screamed.

"*Heeeeeelp!*"

But I knew nothing could save me this time.

Because the three green claws were turning, preparing to seize my throat.

And I couldn't take a single step to escape their murderous grasp!

Chapter Nineteen

As the huge green claws slowly grew toward me, I remembered one of Mom's lessons about jungle plants.

I recognized that these weren't fronds from a real palm tree — they were the branches of a traveler's palm. Their shape was unusual, with many leaves arranged in a fan around one branch.

Mom had said each one of those leaves carried water inside. Maybe, I thought, the water could help me get unstuck somehow.

Mom had been able to clean up a lot of the slime with soap and water, I recalled.

It was worth a try. With the claws closing in, I had nothing to lose.

I ripped off a large leaf and ducked below the approaching plants. I dumped the leaf's water on my left foot, frantically using the stem to scrape away the gunk.

One of the traveler's leaves curled around my neck. I broke loose while still digging at the goo, knowing that the other leaves would grab me in seconds.

It was working. I was almost free now.

But not soon enough!

One of the great claws snatched me around the chest, pulling me toward the tropical forest. As the tree began to drag me through the window, the slime left a trail of thin, sticky strings hanging off my foot.

I had no way to escape. I felt sure I was doomed.

Then I heard something: *Whack!*

I fell safely inside the bedroom.

It was Snake-eye! He'd come back — and sliced off the traveler's palm branch with his hatchet.

"Run, Jason!" he shouted as he hacked at the branches. "Get yourself into the front of the cabin right now, you hear?"

My left foot was still gooey, but I could sort

of run on my toes. I hobbled to Timmy and sat beside him on the couch.

Warily, I watched the plants that now nearly covered the living room windows.

The door suddenly opened — and in walked Snake-eye, carrying his hatchet.

"What on earth have you been up to, boy?" Snake-eye demanded. "I warned you about 'procoharim' but you just went ahead anyway, eh? Was you cutting them trees up or something? You been destroying things out here, boy?"

"No, honest, Snake-eye! We haven't done anything!" I answered. "I have no idea why this is happening! The plants just started attacking us! We didn't hurt anything!"

"Sonny, this don't happen for no reason," Snake-eye said. "I've lived out here a good long while, and I ain't never seen nothing like it! If I weren't seeing all this myself, I wouldn't believe it. Now I want to know . . . "

The sound of shattering glass interrupted us.

First, glass smashed in the bedroom Timmy and I shared.

Then in Mom's room.

Snake-eye ran to see what was wrong.

"It's the trees, boy! They getting so big they's breaking right through the windows," he said. "I'll go chop off their branches, best I can! You two wait right here. OK, Sonny?"

"But Snake-eye! The plants might get you!" I protested. "You can't fight them off alone."

"Sonny, the plants ain't tried to hurt *me* so far, 'cause I ain't never done nothing to hurt *them* — 'til now, that is," Snake-eye replied. "So I figure I got a while longer before they get mad at me, too. You wait with your brother!"

I heard Snake-eye hacking at the attacking plants for several minutes, slicing off branches in both bedrooms. Then he closed both bedroom doors and returned to us, breathing hard.

"Them thin doors ain't gonna hold back the trees for long," he said. "The branches are growing thick and strong so fast it's scaring the daylights out of me. We got to figure out some plan here real quick or we're *all* goners."

"What can we do, Snake-eye?" I asked. My

voice trembled, and I noticed that one of my knees was shaking badly.

Timmy was whimpering.

"It's OK, Timmy," I said, shakily. "We'll be all right."

"I want Mommy," he said, crying and sucking his thumb.

"There's got to be *something* making these plants go crazy like this!" Snake-eye insisted. "Help me here, sonny. Think hard! You must have done something to make this jungle want to wring your necks!"

At that moment, we heard a noise outside — like a loud motor nearby.

Snake-eye looked out the window, but he could see nothing through the dense plants. He tried to open the door but a palm frond darted into the room.

He slammed the door on it, then hacked off the green tip that protruded inside the cabin.

Then a thin branch curled *under* the front door, sliding along the floor toward the couch where Timmy and I huddled together in terror.

I stared at it in horror. I could not breathe.

Snake-eye chopped off the branch. Another one poked under the door. Then another! And another!

"Don't know how long I can hold 'em off like this, sonny! It ain't looking good," he shouted.

He whacked the branches furiously with his hatchet. Sweat poured off him, and he grunted loudly each time he swung.

Branches began to enter under the bedroom doors, wriggling toward the couch. Then the living room windows broke into pieces as vines wormed their way inside.

Snake-eye hacked madly at every plant in sight.

"You boys better get ready to run for all you're worth!" he screamed. "The jungle is taking over! These plants is gonna kill us all!"

Chapter Twenty

Snake-eye flailed at the plants, which seemed to grow from everywhere now.

He was chopping and sweating, running from place to place. But he was losing his fight.

Suddenly, all the branches under the door curled up dead! The front door opened — and Mom walked in! She was carrying three laboratory bottles with silver liquid in them.

She tossed some of the liquid on the other branches, and they also withered and died.

"*Mom*!" I hollered, jumping up to greet her.

"*Mommy*!" Timmy shouted, running to her.

She slammed the door shut, hugging and kissing us wildly.

"Jason! Timmy! I was so afraid for you boys! I almost couldn't make it from the airboat into the cabin. I dumped this mercury on the plants to kill some of them. But more plants are just growing in their place. This is a nightmare," she said.

She looked up and saw Snake-eye's ugly face, his left eye glaring glassily down at her.

"Who are *you*?" she asked. "Are you the cause of all this madness? What have you done to my sons?"

"That's Snake-eye, Mom," I said. "He saved our lives!"

Mom had no time to thank him before Snake-eye angrily pointed a wrinkled finger at her.

"So it's *you*!" he shouted at her. "*You're* the one that's been doing the destroying around here, ain't you? What're you doing to these plants out here in the 'Glades to turn 'em into killers? You're some kind of scientist, ain't you?"

"Are you crazy? I haven't done a thing to harm the Everglades," Mom responded.

That was the instant when I understood.

It *was* Mom — and her experiments!

Snake-eye was right.

"Your research, Mom! Harvesting the sawgrass to make fertilizer," I shouted at her. "That *must* be it! That's why the plants are attacking! They're just fighting back!"

"No, Jason. That's impossible," Mom answered. "It's completely illogical."

"You was planning to kill sawgrass for *fertilizer*, lady?" Snake-eye hollered. "You must be nuts! Bringing in all kind of machines to knock down these trees around here and then rip up acres of sawgrass? You'd kill the 'Glades for miles around — and everything in it!"

"Well, my . . . uh, good Lord!" Mom sputtered. "No, I didn't . . . that is, I just thought a little fertilizer . . . "

"Well, them trees outside don't need any fertilizer *now*, do they? They's growing fast enough for me!" Snake-eye shouted. "We gotta do something to stop this, lady. You're almost out of that silver liquid of yours — and the plants are coming back for us."

Mom paused a moment to think. She looked sadly at Timmy and me.

"Boys, I'm so sorry about all of this," she

said. "Forgive me. I had no idea anything like this could happen. I didn't want to hurt the Everglades. But I think I know what we have to do now. Come on, let's stick together."

With a whole jungle snapping and grabbing at our bodies, Mom led us out the door toward the airboat. Whenever a tree nearly snagged one of us, she tossed a few drops of mercury on it, shriveling the leaves.

At the same time, Snake-eye swiped at the plants with his hatchet, helping to keep them away.

"We're almost there," Mom said. "Stay close to each other!"

Finally, we made it to the airboat. Everyone climbed inside.

Mom pulled several lab bottles from a black equipment bag, opening them one at a time and dumping the green contents into the Everglades.

"These are my sawgrass samples," she shouted, as if she was announcing it to the jungle. "*All* of them! I don't want them. I don't want to get rich by hurting any living thing, especially some place as beautiful as the Everglades. I swear I will never again do anything to hurt this place — or any plant or animal in it!"

The killer plants suddenly stopped straining to snatch us from the boat.

The vines and leaves no longer wiggled and writhed. The bushes and trees became almost motionless now, only swaying slightly in the hot Florida breeze.

The jungle attack was over.

Our family would survive this Everglades vacation after all.

"Good work, Mom!" I shouted. "You did it!"

"You done good, lady," Snake-eye said. "Guess everyone's entitled to make a mistake. Only this mistake almost cost us our lives. Hope you learned something from all this."

"It won't happen again, I can assure you of that, sir," Mom answered. "Not in the Everglades. Nor anywhere else! What's more, I intend to come back here for research that can help *preserve* this spectacular place. That will be my apology to the environment around here."

Her voice grew softer, and more husky. I thought she was going to cry.

"And my thanks to you, sir," she said quietly, "for saving my sons' lives."

"Your new kind of work would be real nice, lady," Snake-eye said, smiling a wide, gap-toothed grin. "Just don't do it 'round here, all right? Take your research to another part of the 'Glades. That's all the thanks I need."

"Yeah, and next time, come back without *us*, huh Mom?" I said, smiling and patting Timmy on the head. "I don't think I want to see this jungle again for a while. And I know Timmy doesn't want to see it. Right Timmy?"

"I want to go home, Mommy," Timmy babbled, tugging at Mom's pants. "I want to go home!"

"We're going to go back inside for our things, then leave right away, boys," Mom said. "The airboat will carry us back to our car, and we'll start driving for Kansas tonight. We'll be home in two days."

"Wow, that sounds great!" I cried, as we hurried toward the cabin to pack. "I can't wait. Kansas City, here I come!"

"Kansas? So you folks is from Kansas, eh?" Snake-eye asked. "Well, guess you found out you wasn't in Kansas no more. Things in the 'Glades is real different."

"Yes, and I think we learned another lesson on this trip," Mom replied. "Didn't we, Jason? You understand what I'm talking about, don't you?"

She looked at me with a smile and winked. It took me a second but finally I got her little joke.

"Sure, Mom. It's hard to forget this lesson when you're from Kansas," I answered with a laugh. "We learned there's no place like home! There's *no* place like home! *There's no place like home!*"

THE AWFUL
APPLE ORCHARD

DANIEL AND HIS LITTLE SISTER SARA
ARE ALLOWED TO MISS SCHOOL FOR A
TWO-WEEK VACATION WITH THEIR
PARENTS IN A CABIN IN THE CATSKILLS.
THEIR FATHER MENTIONS RUMORS
THAT THE LOCAL APPLE ORCHARD AND
CIDER MILL ARE HAUNTED. BUT, WHEN
STRANGE THINGS START HAPPENING,
DANIEL AND SARA BEGIN TO THINK THE
STORY WAS MORE THAN JUST A RUMOR.
WORSE, THEY HAVE REASON TO
BELIEVE THAT NO ONE WILL BELIEVE
THEM—AND SARA MAY BE IN VERY
GRAVE DANGER.